Dory Dory Black Sheep

DORY
FANTASMAGORY

Dory Dory Black Sheep

ABBY HANLON

Dial Books for  Young Readers

To the Kerney farm

DIAL BOOKS FOR YOUNG READERS
Penguin Young Readers Group
An imprint of Penguin Random House LLC
375 Hudson Street | New York, New York 10014

Copyright © 2016 by Abby Hanlon

CIP Data is available.
ISBN 9781101994269

Printed in the United States of America
5   7   9   10   8   6

Designed by Jennifer Kelly
Text set in Albertina MT Std

BLACK SHEEP

a member of a family or group
who does things a little differently

CHAPTER 1
Such a Baby Book

My name is Dory but everyone calls me Rascal. I have a lot of freckles. My hair is just messy. This is my nightgown that I try to wear as much as I can.

But the most important thing about me is that I have two worlds. One is real and one is imaginary.

This is my real world:

This is my imaginary world:

My two worlds swirl together like a chocolate and vanilla ice-cream cone. Real and unreal get all mixed up into one crazy flavor. And things are always happening to me! But my brother and sister just say I'm annoying. And they say I eat gross.

Every morning, Luke and Violet build a wall of cereal boxes around me so they can't see me eat.

"I just can't watch her slurping up her soggy cereal," says Luke.

"I just can't look at the milk dripping down her chin," says Violet. "Augck!"

But I'm not listening to them. Because Mrs. Gobble Gracker is on the back of my cereal box. I don't know what it says, but I can tell it's bad news.

Then my mom comes in the kitchen and starts screaming her head off.

RASCAL! YOU AREN'T DRESSED YET?

But before I get dressed, I have to wake up Mary. Lately, I've had to wake her up with a pan in my hand so she knows *I really mean it*. She's gotten super lazy now that she stays home when I'm at school.

I try to think of things that Mary can do while I'm gone.

Can you make 150 wet toilet-paper balls and put them under Violet's bed?

I don't want
her to feel left out.

At least she's happy when I brush her fur.

On the walk to school, I invent a new game. It's called "Don't Step on the Sticky Poij." The Poij is poisonous gum. And if you step on it, it drains the blood out of your heart.

RASCAL! YOU FORGOT YOUR BACKPACK!

Good-bye hug?

"It's everywhere! It's moving! It's alive!" I shout. "And Luke stepped on it!"

"No, I didn't," yells Luke.

"It's on your shoe!"

"There's nothing there."

"Help! Help!" I scream. "My brother is losing blood." I jump on Violet.

"We need a doctor!" I yell. "Are you a doctor?" I ask the little boy ahead of us.

But as soon as I see Rosabelle in the school-yard, I forget all about the Poij.

Rosabelle has a big thick chapter book in her lap. She looks up and sees me running toward her.

We take turns picking each other up. It's like hugging, but more dangerous.

It's fun to pick up Rosabelle because she is so poufy. She wears six skirts under her dress! She also wears a sparkly headband on her forehead, which she says is her crown. She has little tiny heels on her shoes that go *clickety-click* on the playground. Today she has flowers stuck in her headband that look like she made them out of tissues.

"I love pretending to read chapter books, too!" I say as I grab her book and open it. "Now, *this book* is great for kids but totally inappropriate for grown-ups. Kids, listen! Grown-ups, cover your ears!"

Rosabelle thinks I'm funny.

Then it's time to go inside.
I love my classroom
because Rosabelle sits
right next to me. On the
other side of me is George.

While Rosabelle is
busy drawing, George
says, "Raise your hand if
you ever found a Lego in
your underwear!"

Then George whispers, "Raise your hand if your mom ever told you to shut up!"

George and I raise our hands.

"Raise your hand if you ever hurt your thumb dancing," says George.

Just George raises his hand.

"Raise your hand if . . ." but our teacher interrupts because it's time for morning meeting.

After we do all the boring stuff (count the days we've been in school with straws, make tally marks for the weather, and put a sticker on today's date on the calendar) our teacher tells us, "Today is an exciting day in our class. Everyone is going to get a reading partner. You and your partner are going to be reading the same books together every day during reading time! And you'll have wonderful conversations about what you read!"

I raise my hand right away.

"Can Rosabelle be my partner?"

"Well, you don't get to choose your partner," she says. "Your partner is going to be someone who is reading at the same level as you."

"Great!" I say. "Rosabelle and I are on the same level about everything. We are even the same height, we sit at the same table, we play the same games . . . let me think, I'm sure there's more . . ."

"Dory," my teacher interrupts. "Not now."

"Oh," I say.

When it's time for reading partners, I show Rosabelle that I'm crossing my fingers, legs, and arms for good luck. AND TONGUE!

The teacher calls our names. "When you hear your name, go find your partner."

But when I hear her say "Dory and George," I uncross all my wishes and sink down into my chair.

George hears our names just as he returns to the classroom from the bathroom. With a *huge* grin on his face, he runs up to me, but on his way he trips on a chair. Just as he crashes into me, he *kisses my arm!*

"Gross!" I say. "Don't kiss me!"

"Sorry," he says. "It was an accident."

"You can't kiss someone by accident!" I say.

"I did! I fell down just when my lips were already smooched up like this! Like I was *about to* kiss someone!"

"Don't do that again," I say in my grumpiest voice.

"Okay, partner," he says.

"I wanted Rosabelle to be my partner," I say quietly.

"But then you'd have to read big, thick, boring old books," he says.

I look over at Rosabelle. She has the same chapter book that she had this morning. And Clara, her reading partner, has the exact same book!

I walk over to them. "Can you read that book for real?" I ask Rosabelle. "By yourself?"

"Uh-huh," she says. "I read in my head."

I'm so surprised I just stand there, with my mouth open. No sound comes out.

"It's really easy," says Clara, and then turns to Rosabelle. "What chapter are you up to?"

"Chapter six," says Rosabelle.

"Oh my goodness! Me too!" says Clara.

I go back to my reading spot with a lump in my throat like I'm about to cry.

George and I have a red basket of Easy Reader books. I take them out of the bin one by one. "This one is about farm animals . . . this one is about farm animals . . . farm animals . . . farm animals. . . . Every single one of these books is about farm animals! These books are terrible!" I say.

"Yeah, and I can't even read them!" says George.

Our teacher comes over. "I think you two are going to love this new series I chose for you. It's called Happy Little Farm."

We pretend we are reading until she leaves.

"If I was the farmer, I would just eat all the animals," whispers George.

"If I was the farmer, I would move to the city, and get an apartment with an elevator," I say.

"If I was the farmer, I would run around naked and put mud all over my body and then stick things to it," says George.

"But you would do that anyway," I say.

"Yeah . . ." he says.

I flip through the pages of the book. "This is such a baby book!" I say. "But look, this little black sheep is kind of cute." I show George the picture.

"And he's looking at you," George says.

"What do you mean?" I say, and hold the book up closer.

"I think his name is Goblin," I say.

"Does it say that?" George asks.

"I don't know," I say. "I can't read."

"Raise your hand if you hate reading!" says George.

And we both raise our hands high in the air.

CHAPTER 2
One Tiny Mistake

On the walk home, I don't even care about the Sticky Poij. Because all the blood is drained out of my heart already.

"Geez, why is Rascal in such a bad mood today?" asks Luke.

When I get
home, the only
thing I'm in the
mood to do is
this:

"Dory, what are you doing? DON'T!" yells
my mom. "STOP!"

"Okay . . . you said, 'Don't Stop,'" I say, and
keep doing it.

"You know what I meant!" she yells. "You
are going to end up in the emergency room.
Give me those hammers right now."

My mom grabs the hammers and I give her one big growl before I let go. Then she puts them up high where I can't reach.

"I'm starving!" I say. "Can I have a bunch of cake?"

"How about some yogurt?" she says.

She always says yogurt! I follow her into the

27

kitchen. Luke and Violet are doing their home-work, so I sneak up and pinch them *because they deserve it.*

"It feels good!" says Luke.

"Then I'll do it harder!" I say in an evil voice.

"Hey, have you ever noticed Rascal always pinches with her mouth open?" asks Luke.

"How interesting," says Violet. "Hey, Rascal . . . pinch me."

But each time I pinch her, my mouth opens no matter how hard I try to keep it shut. Now Luke and Violet can't stop laughing.

"Dory, don't *you* have homework, too?" asks my mom, leading me away from them. "Your backpack looked pretty heavy today."

"Oh yeah," I mumble. I put on my backpack and head upstairs.

I'm going to need PRIVACY!

"That sounds just super," my mom hollers back.

In my backpack, I have every book from the red basket. I'm going to learn to read them all today so that I can be partners with Rosabelle! I decide to read in the bathroom because there's a lock on the door. I don't want Luke and Violet to find out about my baby books.

"Come on." I grab Mary. "We're hanging out in the bathroom today. Get in here."

"Can I take a bath?" asks Mary.

"Fine. Go for it," I say.

I spread the books out on the bathroom floor.

The cows love to eat grass. They are happy.

The pigs love to eat corn. They are happy.

"The cow . . . low-vee to eee-yat . . . g-g-g . . . something? Gar-bage? There are hey-pee . . .?"

"The pig low-vee to eee-yat kr-kr . . . crackers? This? are . . . hey-pee?" I try a few more pages. This book makes NO sense!

"What the heck is hey-pee?" asks Mary.

"Who knows! Who writes these books anyway?"

Just then, we hear a *knock knock* on the bathroom door.

"Who's there?" I ask.

"*Baaaa who?*" says Mary.

No answer.

"I'll get it," I say, but when I try to turn the lock, it won't move. "Oh my gosh! Oh no! I can't open it. The lock won't turn! Help! This lock is stuck! Let me out! Let me out!!" I scream and bang on the door.

I can hear voices downstairs, but no one is coming to my rescue.

"HELP!!! HELP!!!" I scream over and over again.

I hear my mom say, "I think I hear Rascal. Can one of you go check on her please?"

"LET ME OUT!!" I scream. "I NEVER EVEN HAD SNACK!"

"Oh, she's just yelling about something," I hear Luke say. "She's fine."

As I'm screaming and banging, I don't notice there's a sheep sliding under the door like a pancake.

"Ahhhhh!!!!" screams Mary.

"You're scared of a lamb?"

"I'm not scared of any lamb . . . I'm scared of
that lamb . . . 'cause he's FLAT!"

"Shhhh! Calm down!" I say, and fluff the
lamb up again. "It's Goblin. He belongs in one
of these farm books."

"Well, how did he get out?" screams Mary.

"I don't know, these things happen when you read, I mean . . . when you can't read."

"Well, put him back!" yells Mary.

"Okay . . . then it looks like we are going to have to read the old-fashioned way," I say, opening one of the books on the floor.

"What does that mean?" asks Mary.

"I just made it up. It means we're going IN the book."

"I'm not getting out of this tub," says Mary.

"Does this look familiar?"

I ask Goblin. "No?"

I see a farmer on the next page. "Maybe that's where you belong. Come on, let's go."

But Goblin just looks
up at me with his lost and
lonely eyes and sticks close
by my side. I hear
the farmer calling
my name.

It's Mr. Nuggy, my fairy godmother!

"Mr. Nuggy!" I yell, running toward him.

"Farmer Nuggy here," he says. "How nice to
see you! Great lookin' sheep you got there!"

"Huh??? *You're a farmer?* But can you still do
magic?" I ask.

"Of course!" he says. "What do you need?"

"*I need to read!* Can you do some magic and turn me into a reader?" I ask him.

"*A reader?* Why, what a beautiful, exciting thing to be! Oh, the worlds you will discover! The adventures that await you! The pages and pages of dreamlands you'll sail through!"

NO WAY. Dory is not going any-where!

"Great. Can you do it now because I'm kind of in a rush," I say. "I've got a sheep to return."

"Okay, wait right here. I'll go mix up the ingredients for your Magic Reading Potion," he says, and walks into the barn.

But while I'm waiting, a horrible surprise pops out from behind the haystack. "Dory, Dory, Dory!" says Mrs. Gobble Gracker.

"*Mrs. Gobble Gracker?* What are YOU doing at Mr. Nuggy's farm? Are you stealing that sheep?" I ask her.

"Yes, I am."

But Mrs. Gobble Gracker grabs the potion from him with a mean old trick.

"Dory is a baby. She can't learn to read! If Dory grows up, that would ruin all my fun, wouldn't it?" asks Mrs. Gobble Gracker, holding my potion. "Don't you remember? Dory is a baby FOREVER! *Just like her little pet lamb here.*"

"He's not my pet!"

"Say good-bye to your silly little potion," says Mrs. Gobble Gracker. "MMMmmmm. This smells good. Is there coffee in it?"

Then in one gulp she drinks the whole thing.

MINE!

She licks her lips.

Suddenly, Mrs. Gobble Gracker tips over a little. She drops the sheep and grabs my arm. She says, "I don't feel well. That potion made my stomach woopy. I feel so hot . . . I've got to go home. My head is spinning." Then she says a bunch of *really weird stuff.*

I feel like I'm shrinking!
My clothes are too itchy.
I want candy! I'm not tired!
Are we there yet? I want it NOW!
Why? But why?
I'm telling . . .

Waaa! Waaa! My sandwich broke!

And then she stumbles away.

"HOLY COW. *What's going on?*" I ask Farmer Nuggy. "Is this what happens when you learn how to read?"

"Definitely not," he says, looking very worried. "I must have made a mistake with the recipe. One tiny mistake and you can get a totally different potion."

"So what's happening to her?" I ask.

"It could be anything," he says.

"What do you mean *anything*? Like she could be turning into a potato?"

"Even mashed potatoes," says Mr. Nuggy. "Even a French fry! Potato salad! The sky is the limit. Magic is an endless power!"

"Okay, um, thanks anyway," I say. "But I think I'll learn how to read the regular old way."

Finally, I hear footsteps coming up the stairs, so I smush myself against the bathroom door. "LET ME OUT! LET ME OUT!" I yell.

"Dory! Are you locked in the bathroom *again?*" asks my mom.

"Uh-huh."

"I've told you—I don't know how many times—you have to turn the lock to the left, *toward the sink.* That's it!"

Oh . . . yeah. *Click.*

"Rascal! What is going on in this bathroom?" my mom asks. "What happened in
here? And why are there books all over the
floor? Were you taking a bath?"

"I was just reading," I tell my mom.

"Really? You were? That's . . . wonderful!" she says.

"I got into the book," I say.

"I just love when that happens," she says, and gives me a hug.

That night before bed, my dad reads my favorite book to me.

Later when my mom tucks me in she asks, "Why did you come home from school in such a bad mood?"

I tell my mom the truth. "I don't think Rosabelle will want to be friends with me anymore. 'Cause I'm such a bad reader."

"Don't be silly. I'm pretty sure Rosabelle can see *there's no one else like you*," says my mom.

As I fall asleep, I wonder if my mom is right.

CHAPTER 3
Everywhere That Dory Went

On the walk to school the next morning, I suddenly have a funny feeling. "Wait," I tell Luke and Violet and grab their arms. "Stop right here! Don't move a muscle!"

"SHUT UP ABOUT THE STICKY POIJ!" they both yell at me at the same time.

"No, it's not that, it's something else."

Then I whisper, "I think I'm being followed by a lamb."

"Did she say a lamb?" Violet asks Luke.

"Yeah, I did, *husssshhhh*."

Violet laughs. Then she sings, "*And everywhere that Dory went, Dory went, Dory went, everywhere that Dory went, the lamb was sure to go.*"

"I said *husssshhhh*!"

Luke sings, "*He followed her to school one day, school one day, school one day, he followed her to school one day, which was against the rule.*"

"Wait for me," I tell them, and go look behind the bushes.

"HOLD ON! Give me one sec!" I yell, looking in some garbage cans. "It was a little black sheep," I say.

"The only black sheep that is following us is YOU!" says Violet.

"Okay, I was wrong," I say.

But when I get to the school yard ... there he is. I knew it! *Don't wave at me, please don't wave at me, please don't wave at me.* Why do these things *always* happen to me?

Then Goblin starts sniffing my backpack, and I realize he must be hungry. So, I give him some of my salami sandwich. And what the heck, I'll have some, too.

Rosabelle comes running over. "Rascal! Why are you eating your lunch before school again?"

"I'm not eating it *all*. I'm sharing with . . ." I start to say but then stop. I don't want to tell Rosabelle that a lamb escaped from my embarrassing babyish farm book.

"Oh, never mind," I say.

"Oh," she says, and looks disappointed.

But when I see Clara walking over to us, I quickly change my mind. "I'm being followed," I whisper.

"Uuuuuuhhhh! Really? Is it Mrs. Gobble Gracker?" she asks. *"Is she back?"*

"No, it's a little black sheep named Goblin."

"Hi, Rosabelle!" says Clara. "Guess what? I'm on chapter ten already! 'Cause I read four more chapters last night!"

"Really?" says Rosabelle. "Wow. That's a lot. Hhhhmmm . . . a black sheep named Goblin? Do you think he's a spy? Do you think he's dangerous?"

"Sheep? There's no sheep in this book, is there?" asks Clara. "Wait a minute, are you ahead of me, *did you read more than me last night?*"

"Huh?" says Rosabelle. "I don't think so."

"Actually, he's kind of cute," I tell Rosabelle.

"Really? No fair!" says Rosabelle. "I want a cute lamb to follow me!"

At reading time, I have no partner because George stuck his finger in the pencil sharpener. And the teacher is busy trying to get it out.

So it's the perfect time to sneak over to Rosabelle. I pretend I'm looking for something in the closet, so I can be near Rosabelle's reading spot. But when I hear Clara and Rosabelle talking about their book, I just stop and listen:

"I feel sooooo bad for Hannah when she starts to cry!"

"Yeah, why is Henry so mean to her?"

"I think he doesn't like girls."

"I love Hannah. She's smart. Besides, I think she is going to solve the mystery without Henry's help. Remember when she went through the haunted castle alone?"

"But how will she get past the three-headed monster?"

"Well, she does have her own sword!"

"But she has a broken leg!"

Listening to them, I've never been so jealous in my life. I would chop off my right arm to be able to read that book.

In the closet I sink into a pile of backpacks.

Before I get in trouble for being in the closet again, I go back to my desk. "Why did you stick your finger in the pencil sharpener?" I ask George.

"'Cause I thought I could miss ALL of reading, but I only missed SOME of reading," he says. "But it was fun anyway!" He smiles and holds up his bandaged finger. Then he says, "Guess what! I had a dance party last night!

And I invented this new kind of dance we can do when we're bored during reading. It's called the Mini-Dance. Watch."

Then George does a little dance with his hands.

"Shhh," I say, opening my book. "We have to read."

"Come on, let's read together," says George.

"Fine, you can come with me," I say. "But I've got a sheep to return, so this is serious business."

"Where are we?" asks George.

"Just stick with me, I've been here before," I tell him.

We come to a bunch of signs, but we can't read them.

"How about this way?" asks George.

"All right," I say. "Let's go!"

"Hmm, we're still at a farm, nothing too different. Well, maybe it's a little different," says George.

"Look! Someone is coming over to us," says George.

"Hi. I'm Gigi. Can I play with your sheep?" says a little girl with a super-scratchy voice.

Gigi stares at us, waiting for an answer, but we don't know what to say. There is something strange about her ... but also familiar.

"Watch!" she says. "There are so many ways to play!" Then she climbs on Goblin. Goblin is furious!

He runs in crazy circles around us until Gigi gets thrown off. She lands in a bucket of water. While Gigi is stuck in the bucket, I give Goblin a little pat—he's even softer than he looks.

When I pet him, he closes
his eyes and licks my leg.

Gigi crawls out of the bucket and says,
"Want a cup of coffee?"

"Sure." George shrugs.

I give him a little kick. "Ow! Why'd you kick
me?" he asks.

"We don't want coffee," I say. For some reason, I do not trust this girl at all.

Gigi takes a big gulp of her coffee. "Listen, I'll make a deal with you. I'll give you a huge jar of pickles if I can have your sheep . . . for keeps."

"Those don't look like pickles," says George.

"They're pickled spiders, dummy," says Gigi.

"No deal," I say.

"Why not?" asks George. "This is your chance to get rid of that sheep!"

"I changed my mind," I say, and pick up Goblin.

"Oh phooey," says Gigi, and kicks some dirt. "Well, what do you want to do then?" she asks.

"'Cause I want to play with your sheep! We could give him bubbly water and see what happens! I already know what happens . . . it's *really* funny. Have you ever put pants on a sheep? Want to do it? Or, we could just throw rocks at each other if you want? Wait! Are you hungry? Do you want to make chicken soup?"

Gigi runs inside the barn and comes out with a big pot and spoon. She chases the chickens and yells, "Hey, chickens! Hop in the pot!"

"Lost in a good book?" says my teacher, standing over me. She does not look happy.

How did she know we were lost, I wonder.

"Dory and George, I noticed you were playing during reading time today."

Then she says, "And Rosabelle, what are you doing over here? Go back to your reading spot right now please."

Rosabelle? What is she doing hiding under the desks?? Was *she* spying on *me?*

Slowly, Rosabelle walks back to her reading spot.

After reading, we line up for gym. Rosabelle rushes to line up next to me. "I figured it out! Gigi is Mrs. Gobble Gracker! As *a kid!*" I try to look scared, but I can't help smiling because *I love this game.*

"But how did Mrs. Gobble Gracker get five hundred years younger?" asks Rosabelle.

I whisper in Rosabelle's ear, "She drank the wrong potion."

"I just can't believe it!" says Rosabelle. "I'm in shock. I think I'm going to faint."

CHAPTER 4
Twenty Minutes Every Day

When I get home from school, I grab a banana to call Farmer Nuggy.

"What do you need? More potatoes?" he asks.

"No, I'm fine. Hey, listen, do you know that your potion turned Mrs. Gobble Gracker into a kid named Gigi?"

"*A kid?*" he asks. "Oh dear! I must have used a little too much vinegar."

"And guess what? She wants to *play with me!!*"

"With *you?*" asks Farmer Nuggy, and then he starts laughing. He is laughing so hard that I can't understand what he is saying. I think he said he peed in his pants.

"It's not funny! I'm hanging up!" I say.

"Wait!" I hear him say just as I put the banana down.

I jump off the counter and am walking out of the kitchen when the banana rings. "Can you get it?" I ask Mary.

Tell Dory that the potion will wear off. It doesn't last! It will only work for a few days and then Mrs. Gobble Gracker will be back to normal. So be careful! Okay, I have to hang up, my pants are wet. Don't forget!

Okey-dokey.

Upstairs in my room, I find Goblin sitting right in the middle of my bed. *That's it! I'm keeping this sheep!* He can sleep in my closet. He can have my sleeping bag! I didn't choose this sheep, but this sheep chose me! I give him a little kiss on the head.

"There you go, nice and safe. Need anything else? A cookie? A song? I know! I'll go get you a bowl of water!"

On my way out, I run into Mary. "Farmer Nuggy told me to tell you that the po—" she says. But my mom is right behind her.

My mom interrupts Mary. "It's reading time," she says, standing at my door.

"No, no, no, no, please!" I say. "I'm busy. Not now."

"Every day after school you need to read to me for twenty minutes. That's your home-work. And it's getting late."

"Can I just get a bowl of water?"

"A *bowl* of water? No! Come on! Let's read on the couch."

And then the phone rings. My mom gets up to answer it. While she's gone, I quickly run upstairs to get Goblin a bowl of water.

Hhmmmm... What was I supposed to tell her again?

Then just before my mom comes back, I hide the book in my pants.

"Guess what? That was Rosabelle's dad," she says. "Rosabelle wants you to come over after school tomorrow."

I stare at my mom in disbelief. "To her castle?" I say. "I've been invited to her castle?"

"Dory, just because Rosabelle likes to pretend to be a princess, doesn't mean she lives in a castle, you know that. Now, where's that book we were reading?"

"To her castle?" I say again. "TO THE CASTLE!" I shout.

Then I spin and spin all around. What else is there to do with all this happiness?

"Is that the book in your pants? Ugh! Forget it," says my mom. *"I'm making dinner."*

At dinner, I tell Luke and Violet my big news. "If anyone is looking for me after school tomorrow, I'll be at Rosabelle's."

I wait for them to react. Nothing.

"*THEE Rosabelle,*" I say in my fanciest voice.

Still nothing.

I try again. "Rosabelle . . . you know, my friend who lives *in a castle?* Did you know that Rosabelle can draw a 3-D cabbage? And *she said* if you can draw a 3-D cabbage, you can draw anything!"

Still nothing.

"Does anyone in this family care about cabbages?" I shout.

"I care about cabbages," says my dad.

That night I can't sleep. "What do you think her castle looks like inside?" I ask my parents.

Without opening her eyes, my mom says, "How many times are you going to come in here and ask me that?"

"Do you think that at the end of a very long hallway there is a *tiny* little secret golden door that leads to Rosabelle's bedroom? Does her ceiling have those drippy lights that are actually real candles and diamond necklaces? And is her bed so high up like in *The Princess and the Pea*? And there's probably a ladder to get up. And a slide to get down! And at the bottom of the slide, she has fluffy pink bunny slippers that are perfectly lined up, just waiting there for her to wake up! And—"

"If you can't sleep, why don't you try counting sheep?" mumbles my dad.

"Sheep? Why would I count . . . *SHEEP!!* Ahhh! I forgot!" I run out of their room.

I open my closet door and count "One sheep," nice and cozy and warm.

CHAPTER 5
Captain Puff

Rosabelle's dad picks us up after school. On the walk home, we jump into puddles, over the Sticky Poij, and I tell Rosabelle all about my new pet sheep. When we get to Rosabelle's house, there's definitely not a moat to cross. Strange.

A little boy in a Batman costume runs to open the door for us.

"RO-RO is home!" he screams, and hugs Rosabelle.

"This is my little brother, Ridley," says Rosabelle.

"HEY! Who are you?" says Ridley, pointing at me.

"Dory," I say.

"She looks like a dumb bear!" Ridley screams, still pointing at me.

My mouth drops open. "What did you say?"

"Ridley!" says their dad, "That is very rude!"

"*She does!*" Ridley continues. "She really does. She looks like a dumb bear."

"Forget him," says Rosabelle. "He's four. He's crazy...."

"What's going on?" Rosabelle's mom calls from her office. "Hi, Dory, nice to meet you! Welcome!" I look around Rosabelle's house. It looks *sort of* like my house, but only when our house gets really messy. Not one thing castle about it.

As I'm walking up the stairs to Rosabelle's room, Ridley points at me and screams, "She ate my chicken nugget!"

"What?" I say.

"That bear ate my chicken nugget!"

"I did not! I just got here! *What is he talking about?*"

Then he starts this terrible annoying cry, *"She ate my chicken nugget!"*

Finally, we are safely away from him in Rosabelle's room with the door shut. But I can still hear him crying downstairs, *"She ate my chicken nugget!"* while Rosabelle's parents try to calm him down.

Rosabelle's room is not exactly *The Princess and the Pea*. It is *the biggest mess* I have ever seen.

I can't even walk without stepping on a Lego.
Her bed is covered with books, and her sheets
and blankets and pillows and skirts are on the
floor *in a nest.*

"Um . . . do you want me to help you clean
up your room?" I ask.

"No thanks," she says, hugging her dragon.

"Are you sure?" I say. "I don't mind."

"We can just shove everything over," she says, and gets on her hands and knees and makes a clearing. Then she sets up a little tea set with water. "Now that Mrs. Gobble Gracker is a kid, anything could happen," she says, and sips her water with her pinkie up. "What if she becomes the new kid at school? Or what if she moves next door to you and your mom makes you play with her?"

"Mrs. Gobble Gracker is so sneaky, I bet Gigi is even sneakier!" I say.

"Wait!" she says. "I just remembered— whatever you do, *don't say anything about Mrs. Gobble Gracker in front of Ridley*," says Rosabelle. "I do NOT want him to know about her! He always copies me and ruins everything, and it's not fair. Okay?"

"Okay," I say.

Suddenly, Ridley bursts into Rosabelle's room and starts taking off his Batman costume until he is down to his fire engine underwear.

"What are you doing? *Get out!!*" says Rosabelle.

He hands the costume to me and says in a creepy robot voice, "YOU. WEAR. IT."

"NO," says Rosabelle. "She's not wearing it."

"How about . . . let's just see if it fits," I say, because I actually kind of want to wear it.

"Really?" says Rosabelle.

It's *a lot of work* to get it on because it's *super tight,* and the mask feels like it's going to shrink my brain, but when I get it on . . . WOW! Something about this costume *just feels awesome.*

"Come on! Let's go back to our teatime!" says Rosabelle.

But now that I'm wearing this costume, I can't stop jumping off her bed.

"I want to fly!!!"

"Yes, I see that," Rosabelle says. "Actually, that's a great idea. Batman can fight Gigi! What are your superpowers?"

"How about underwater breathing and . . . *cross dimensional awareness*?" I ask.

"Let's keep this simple. How about super strength and super speed?" she says. "Don't worry, I'll train you."

"Okay, sure," I say.

"Let me write that down. Wait a minute, do you want to be called Batman or something else?" she asks.

"Hmmm," I say. "Good question."

"Batwoman?" suggests Rosabelle.

"How about . . . how about . . . how about . . . Captain Puff?" I ask.

"CAPTAIN PUFF!" shouts Rosabelle, jumping up and down with excitement. "YES!"

I try out my new Captain Puff voice. I say, "Some people don't believe in superheroes because they haven't met . . ."

But then Ridley returns. And he is wearing all my clothes. "Look at me! I'm a hiker! I hike mountains!"

"Those aren't hiking clothes!" I say, standing on Rosabelle's windowsill.

"Yes, they are! I'm a hiker!! Wherever I go, I hike!"

"Fine, go hike. Go on a nice long hike! Hike away!" Rosabelle says, and pushes him into the hallway. "He's never gonna leave us alone. Let's get out of here. We can go do your superhero training in the backyard."

"Watch out below!" I say, jumping off the windowsill.

"Come on," she says, grabbing my cape, "You can jump off the swings."

But on our way out, we find Ridley in the hallway. He is playing with his toy cars wearing only a tutu and socks on his hands.

"Where are my clothes?" I ask him.

"Your hiking clothes?" he asks.

"My regular clothes! Where are they?"

I wait for an answer.

"Did you know I have *two* boxes of magnetic tiles in my classroom?"

"*So what???*" I say.

"He's trying to change the subject," says Rosabelle. "That means he did something really bad." Rosabelle shakes her head and folds her arms. "Hmmm . . . We can ask my parents to help, but I don't think we're going to get them back."

" 'Cause they're wet," says Ridley.

"*Why are they wet?*" I ask.

"Is Sleeping Beauty a boy or a girl?" he asks. Rosabelle is starting to look really mad.

"Forget it, I don't care about my clothes," I say to Rosabelle. "Let's just get *away* from him."

But as we walk away, we hear Ridley's voice. "I had one frog. Mrs. Gobble Gracker came in my room."

Rosabelle and I freeze.

We turn around to listen. "Mrs. Gobble Gracker said, 'That's my frog,' I said, 'NO, that's my frog.' She said, 'THAT'S MY FROG!' And then I said, 'Okay, you take the hiking clothes.'"

At first we are so confused we don't say anything. Then Rosabelle shouts, "YOU LITTLE SPY!" Rosabelle looks so angry that if she were in a comic book, steam would be coming out of her ears.

"Come on, it's okay," I say, trying to pull her away. But her feet are crazy-glued to the ground. And her eyes are all fired up ready to go.

"YOU LITTLE NOSY BEAST!" she shouts, her face bright red. I had no idea Rosabelle could get this angry. I'm pretty sure she is, what my mom calls, "pushed over the edge."

"YOU LITTLE . . . BUTT-BABY! YOU NOBODY-FACED-SHRIVELED-UP-RAISIN-BRAIN!" she shouts.

And then she attacks.

She pins Ridley to the ground and pulls off his sock hands. "I'M GOING TO RIP YOUR SMELLY SHRIMP HEAD AND SMASH IT INTO THROW UP."

This is getting crazy. I don't know what to do.

But Captain Puff does!

"Excuse me. Let Captain Puff handle this, please!" I say in my Captain Puff voice, shoving myself in between them.

"Come with me, boy,"
I say, dragging him into
his bedroom.

"Are you really Captain Puff?" he asks, breathless.

"Can you fit inside this hamper?" I ask him. "Because this is the safest place for you."

"I think so," he says.

"Climb right in, boy," I say, helping him.

As I leave the room, I hear his small muffled voice from the hamper, "Excuse me, Captain Puff? It's sort of uncomfortable because I'm sitting on some wet hiking clothes that fell in the toilet."

When my mom picks me up, she asks me a million questions in the car. "Where was Rosabelle's brother? I thought she had a little brother? And I don't understand how nobody knows where your clothes are? Why did you put that costume—that is clearly *way too small* for you—on in the first place? It's a size three, Rascal! That means it's for *three-year-olds*. How on earth did you get it over your head? I feel terrible that we had to take their costume. We're going to have to cut it off! With scissors.

At least we left them the cape. Rascal, why do you do these things?"

"A hero does good for good," I say in my Captain Puff voice. "Not for glory."

CHAPTER 6
Little Robber

The first thing Violet says to me when she hears that I lost my clothes is, "Let me guess. Mrs. Gobble Gracker took them."

"Yup," I say. "She traded them . . . for a frog. I think that's what happened?"

Then Luke and Violet start to tease me about my costume. They say I have a wedgie. They laugh so hard they can't get up from the floor. I don't know what a wedgie is, but I can tell it has something to do with my butt. This makes me stop feeling like a superhero. I have to sit down so that Luke and Violet can't keep seeing my butt.

I won't get up from the dinner table until I'm sure it's safe.

"Rascal, can you just *let me* help you take off that costume, or are you going to make a *super*

big deal out of it?" calls my mom from the living room. I don't like either choice, so I don't answer. Instead, I wait. And wait. And wait.

From the living room, my mom says, "We should really read together tonight. Remember . . . twenty minutes . . ." That's the last thing she says before she closes her eyes.

When I'm sure she's asleep, and the house is quiet, I sneak upstairs to my room.

"Presenting . . . Captain Puff!" I say, making the grand entrance I had been planning. Then I fly to the top of my dresser.

"Wow!" says Mary. "How did you become Captain Puff?"

"Because *I* had the best playdate ever!" I say.

"I had a playdate, too," says Mary.

"How?" I ask.

"Gigi came over," she says.

"Gigi??" I jump down from my dresser. "Did you say Gigi?????"

Gigi!?

"She rang the doorbell," says Mary.

"And you let her in????"

"She said she wanted to play."

"What did you play?" I ask.

"Well, first she just wanted to make coffee, so we did that."

"Yeah, and . . . then?"

"She drank a lot of coffee. A LOT."

"Okay . . ."

"So she got *really hyper*."

"What does that mean exactly?" I ask.

"Well, her eyes kind of bugged out and she started talking really fast and running around and touching everything. She banged into A LOT of things, and then she started doing cartwheels, although she's HORRIBLE at them. She couldn't even get her legs up. And then she banged on the piano and sang songs I've never heard of. I think she made them up. They were pretty weird.

"And then she found a HUGE AMOUNT of Post-its in the kitchen drawer and she ran around and stuck them all over the house, in every room . . . on the windows, the walls, the furniture, on the phone . . . everywhere! And then she asked for a snack, but she was *really picky* about everything I offered her. She said

119

she wanted soup, and I said, 'We don't have any soup right now,' and then she threw a big fit, but in the middle of her fit, she got distracted by some crumbs on the kitchen floor and she started playing with them and talking to them in this very high baby voice, and then all of a sudden she ran upstairs to go to the bathroom. She was gone so long I thought she fell in the toilet, but when I came upstairs to look for her, she was gone. Your bedroom window was open. She must have climbed down the side of the house; I guess that's how she likes to leave."

"Where are the Post-its?" I ask.

"I cleaned them all up," says Mary, smiling proudly.

"Wow. Mrs. Gobble Gracker is really a bonkers kid. What did you think?" I ask.

"It was so fun! I loved it!" says Mary. "I *loved loved loved* it! Can she come back tomorrow? Pretty please with a chair on top?"

"It's 'cherry,'" I say.

"I already invited her," says Mary.

And then I remember Goblin. I jump up and open the closet.

The closet is empty.

"Where's Goblin?" I ask Mary.

"I didn't take him out," she says.
"I promise!"

"Then where'd he go?"

"I have no idea," says Mary.

"It was Gigi!" I say. "*That sheep stealer!* I bet she snuck him out the window! I was right! Never trust a Gobble Gracker!"

The next morning at school, I tell Rosabelle and George the news.

"Gigi came to my house, went into my room, and stole my pet sheep!"

"That little thief!" says Rosabelle.

"She's going to put pants on him!" says George.

"Pants?" says Rosabelle. "Who cares about pants? She could be making lamb stew out of him!!"

"What do I do?" I ask them.

"This is your chance, Rascal!" says Rosabelle. "You have to use your superhero powers to battle Gigi and save your sheep!" she says. "Oh . . . *if only you still had the Captain Puff costume, that would be perfect.*"

"Look," I say, and unbutton my shirt so they can see. "My mom fell asleep and forgot about it."

Rosabelle gasps. "You're a genius!"

"That looks *really* uncomfortable,"

says George.

That afternoon, George can't wait to battle Gigi. He keeps raising his hand and asking if it's quiet reading time yet, and the teacher keeps looking over at the pencil sharpener nervously.

When it's finally reading time, George opens his book and says, "Captain Puff! You fly over the barn and grab the sheep! I'll do my karate moves on Gigi."

HiYa!

Just as I reach Goblin, I hear a voice. "Dory, can you read out loud to me for a few minutes?" asks my teacher.

Uh-oh.

"Dory, are you there?" I feel a hand on my shoulder. "I'd love to hear you read," says the teacher, who pulls up a chair next to me.

"Okay," I say.

When I read, the words get all crooked up. The words don't make a story—it's the *opposite* of a story. As I'm reading, I get hotter and hotter and hotter, and my Captain Puff costume feels tighter and tighter underneath my clothes. The teacher writes a whole page in her notebook. Then she pats me on the back and says, "Keep practicing. You'll get there, honey."

When the teacher's gone, I'm quiet. I don't want to play anymore.

"You play without me," I tell George.

"But what are you going to do?" George asks. *"Read?"*

"Yes," I say in a voice so quiet he can't hear me.

That night, after din-
ner and just before bed,
the doorbell rings. I look
out the window and I
see Gigi standing on the
stoop.

I take off my night-
gown. I'm still Captain
Puff underneath.

"Hi, is Mary home?"
asks Gigi when I open
the door.

"You little robber! You
stole my sheep!" I say.

"I know. It was *so fun.*
I was so sneaky! Nobody
saw me!"

With my super strength, I pick up Gigi.
"Give me back my sheep, or I'll fly you straight
out of the universe
and leave you there!"

"That sounds kind
of fun," she says.

So with my super speed, off we go.

"Last chance," I tell her.

GOBLIN?

Goblin walks right past us. "Where is he going?" asks Gigi.

"Look…!" I whisper.

"Is that his family? All those white sheep? It can't be!" says Gigi.

But when we see how much they love him, we know it is. This is where he belongs.

"Oh phooey!" says Gigi, and kicks some space dust.

Good-
bye!

"Um. Can I have a ride back?" asks Gigi.

I could just leave her here. But surrounded by the huge blackness of the universe, I notice how little she is. Maybe even smaller than me.

"Yeah, fine," I grumble.

"That was super weird," says Gigi, sitting on my stoop.

"Yeah, Goblin was *really* lost, huh?"

"He's from another planet!" says Gigi.

"I'll miss him," I say. I sit down next to her.

"He was the greatest sheep I ever stole," says Gigi.

The sky is dark. The stars are out. I take off my mask.

"What do you want to be when you grow up?" I ask Gigi.

"The biggest robber ever! I can't wait to grow up! I bet my nose will get even longer! I want to live in a cave and wear a long black—"

"Shhh. Be quiet for a second," I say.

From the stoop, I can hear my parents' voices through the open window in the living room. They are talking about me!

"Rascal's teacher called today. She says Rascal is going to need extra help with reading," I hear my mom say.

"I'm not surprised," says my dad, laughing. "It's because she never stops talking! How can a person learn to read when they are never quiet for a single second? If she's not talking to us, she's talking to herself!"

"Seriously," says my mom, "I'm concerned. Luke and Violet were reading perfectly by the time they were her age. What are we going to do with her?"

I look at Gigi. I don't want to cry in front of her. But I can't help it.

"I gotta go," says Gigi. "Tell Mary we can play another day."

Upstairs in my room, after a lot of sweat and a couple of rips, I wiggle myself out of my costume.

I put on my nightgown. Without waiting for anyone to tuck me in, I crawl into my bed and fall asleep.

The next morning, I wake up extra early. One by one, I take my favorite books off the bookshelf. All alone, in the quiet of my room, I lie on the floor with my books. As the morning light slowly shines brighter and brighter through my window, I turn the pages and look carefully at the pictures. I look at the words carefully, too, and some of the words . . . I read.

CHAPTER 7
Hide-and-Seek Tag

The next day, when it's time for reading, my teacher says she decided to make "a little change." From now on, I have a new reading partner. And so does George.

I sit down next to my new partner. She turns to me and says, "I love the Happy Little Farm books, don't you?"

"I guess so," I say.

"Which one is your favorite? My favorite book is about the black sheep who gets lost," she says.

"How did you know he was lost?" I ask.

" 'Cause I read the book, silly," she says.

"Can we read it together?" I ask her.

"Sure," she says, smiling.

Later, at recess, Rosabelle is yelling her head off. "Dory! George! Come quick! Look over there."

Gigi is in our school yard. Tangled in a jump rope.

"*What is she doing here?*" asks George.

"Oh no! She sees us!" says Rosabelle.

"Hi, guys!!!" says Gigi. "Want to tie up the pre-K kids with my jump rope?"

"Do you go to this school?" George asks her.

"Nope," she says. "I don't go to school."

"Then why are you here?"

" 'Cause I love recess!" she says. "Don't you want to play with me?"

"NO WAY!" yells Rosabelle.

"Wait," I tell Rosabelle. "It's okay."

First, I untangle Gigi from the jump rope. Then I say, *"Maybe* we'll play, but it depends on the game."

"Let's play hide-and-seek tag!" says Gigi.

"Not it!" says George.

"Not it!" says Rosabelle.

"Not it!" I say.

I'll be it.

"Okay," I say to Gigi. "The stairs will be the base. We'll go hide, and you close your eyes and count to twenty. Then we have to run to the base before you tag us."

We all go run and hide.

From my hiding spot under the bench, I hear Gigi counting.

Abby Hanlon (www.abbyhanlon.com) is a former teacher. Inspired by her students' storytelling, she began to write her own stories for children, and taught herself to draw. She is the author of *Ralph Tells a Story*, *Dory Fantasmagory*, and *Dory Fantasmagory: The Real True Friend*. Abby lives in Brooklyn, New York, with her husband and their two children.